THE

GOLDEN BALLROOM

A SHORT LONDON LOVE STORY
IN EIGHT PARTS

Read Also

Only Jewels

Listen to

Happy Queer Mind

A SELF-HELP PODCAST FOR LGBTQ+ INDIVIDUALS AND THEIR ALLIES

THE

GOLDEN BALLROOM

A SHORT LONDON LOVE STORY
IN EIGHT PARTS

JESS DARNELL

This book was first self-published in February 2020.

It was revised and re-published in April 2021.

DEDICATION

A very special thank-you to

Georgia, Tian, and Lew,

who first heard this story in its entirety,

for their encouragement and friendship.

This story is for Alex, my real-life Thomas.

TABLE OF CONTENTS

The Ballroom

The Golden Ballroom was around the corner from The Savoy. Down a tight alleyway and through two large, oak doors, you were greeted by a small, balding man named Lindsay, who ran the cloak room. He was in a permanent slump and was rather deadpan as he sat behind the half-door, fiddling with his keys. Staring down his spectacles, the lenses magnifying his two black eyes, Lindsay would croak out one or two high-pitched greetings before eventually cracking a very dry joke, accompanied by a sudden smile of breathy, hissing laughter. He was altogether fabulous and revolting at the very same time.

I handed over my favourite London Fog and took my claim token. He smiled and wheezed, "Enjoy yourself, sir."

I nodded, slipping through the red drapes at the side of his desk. The entire establishment was washed in a soft, humming light that accentuated the antiquated wallpaper, and past the drapes was a snug hallway outfitted in red carpet, worn out by the decades of traffic that passed in and out of the ballroom each night. On particularly busy evenings, you might catch a famous duke or duchess, having arrived undercover and tonguing a member of their own sex. On other nights, you could find slender lady-boys leaning against the wall under the red, beaded sconces smoking cigarettes and giggling.

At the end of the corridor hung a small portrait of Virginia Woolf and to the left of the portrait, in the adjacent wall, was another pair of drapes leading to the ballroom. The great oval dance floor, according to Lindsay, had been imported from Greece when the club had opened back in 1909. A thin, gold railing enclosed the dance floor, containing revellers safely upon the elevated oval, and on the other side of this barrier were many small tables and chairs. At the opposite end of the room was a small stage, where a twelve-piece band of funny faces, slim moustaches, and cigarillos hanging between dark lips wailed out the hits of the day, the waltzes of the future, and several of those old tunes that float back into your memories like smoke when you least expect it.

Tonight, the corridor was empty, except for three boys loitering at the end of the hallway. A moustachioed boy was leaning against the wall over another young man wearing a newsboy cap, who sat on the floor with his legs drawn up and holding his ankles. The third boy, a blonde, stood with his back to me. As I parted the first set of drapes and laid eyes on them, the conversation took a slight pause as they clocked me. The sitting one pulled his cap over his eyes and muttered something.

I kept my eyes on the carpet as I walked when the stood one turned to his friends to say something. I had almost passed when my shoulder bumped the back of the blonde.

I stopped short with a quick, "Sorry."

Before me stood an elegant, blonde boy wearing a white, silk shirt and a pair of immaculate, beige trousers that draped and billowed gloriously over an impeccable, Grecian frame.

He wore no tie, leaving the top few buttons of his long shirt open to reveal something shining—a gold necklace. Embarrassed, I swallowed, turning to go.

I could feel my face flushing when the moustached boy came away from the wall, put his arm around the blonde, and called after me, "Got a light for her majesty here?"

My stomach began to churn. I turned back.

He wore a silver pinky ring on the hand dangling by the blonde's chin.

"Actually, I do," I replied, "Want one?"

The blonde smiled, "Yes, please."

As I leaned into him, producing my matchbox, the collar of his shirt fell aside to reveal an ever so delectable inch of his bare chest. I lit his cigarette and he smiled again, taking a drag.

"See you," he said, exhaling smoothly above our heads.

Nervous and smiling like an idiot, I gave a nod to Virginia on the wall and parted the second set of drapes.

THE BOY

A saxophone was wailing out the last few bars of its sensuous, slow waltz as cigarette smoke lazed through the air. I looked for a table near the dance floor and spotted one on the other end of the room, by the stage.

A voice cut through the music, "Henry? That's Henry! Henry!"

A slim, white hand was shaking at me through the smoke. Each finger was adorned with several rings, the wrist with several bangles and an emerald bracelet.

"Henry, baby!" called the voice. I waved

"Pamela," I winced, "how are you?"

She was sat so close to the bandleader that she could have stolen his spatterdashes.

"Sit, sit!" she urged, patting her hand urgently at the seat. "So," she screeched over the music, slumping forward and resting her arm on the table, "tell me *everything*!"

"What is there to tell?" I shrugged. My indifference must have been lost in the atmosphere.

"What do you mean?" She laughed, "I mean *everything*! How's your mother? How's the cat? How's Jack?"

"Oh, mother is mother, Cookie is Cookie, and Jack stopped calling about a week ago."

"Oh, pet," she sighed, lighting her cigarette, "I had such high hopes. He was a handsome fellow."

She suddenly grabbed my arm and exhaled like a locomotive, "Wait a minute! You were seeing a Dan! Am I wrong? Am I wrong about a Dan?"

I nodded, "You are right about a Dan."

She squealed, but I shook my head.

"I was seeing a Dan, but he decided he was finished seeing a Henry."

"Just out of nowhere?" she asked.

"Just out of nowhere," I echoed.

"Ah, Hen. There'll be someone else soon, I'm sure," she sighed, surveying the room, "Men are beasts."

"Sure," I said, checking the crowd for a pair of beige trousers.

I met Pamela on my first night at The Golden when she was making her best effort to drag a delicious young man home to her flat in Holland Park. She had an unfortunate eye for the boys with limp-wrists, and I never had the heart to point out her misjudgments— especially when her misfortune had worked in my favour so frequently. On more than one occasion (and after more than one gin and tonic), the gentleman on her arm at seven had become the gentleman on *my* arm by nine.

She always swatted the air at me.

"You're just too good!" she would laugh, whipping her bejewelled hands around. Her two big eyes were bulging out of her skull, necklaces sparkling in the chandelier light.

"Oh, Pam," I protested, "you're too kind!"

"At any rate," she muttered, tapping her cigarette in the ash tray, "we all know whomever I pick up tonight will end up in your bed, so what's the use in sulking?"

She winked and offered me a smoke, and we sat watching the crowd for a while.

I had few friends at that time in my life, but Pamela was always entertaining, even at her worst.

"I feel, Henry-dear," she said, fluttering her eyelashes, "that I am in dire need of a drink and a dance." She leaned over the table, smirking royally, "Won't you join me?"

She took my hand and pulled me from my seat as the band rolled out the Charleston— the room when mad. Pamela ran to the dance floor, holding her hands at her shoulders, and began to throw her legs about. She was a stormy forest flicking, rolling, and bending in a dark green dress that glittered in the lights.

When the punching, bouncing rhythm sucked Pamela straight into the crowd, I used the opportunity to circumnavigate the dance floor in hopes of finding a partner. I nudged by an attractive waiter who was pouring champagne, but his attention was soon diverted when he realised that he'd drained a glass of fizz into an elderly woman's handbag.

I slipped onto the dance floor, instead.

For several moments, all I saw were shoes. Black brogues and oxfords twinkled together lightly, while little heels and steel-toes hoofed and stomped. At long last, I found an excellent pair of beige shoes with small, silver buckles that I could follow quite easily. They seemed to scatter gracefully over the floor with efficiency and ease. I tried to manage an embellishment of my own at one point and whirled directly into a large man in a brown suit, tripping backwards to step on one of the beige buckles that had educated me so well.

"Sorry!" I shouted, turning around to apologise.

"No trouble, buddy," sang the buckles.

It was the blonde boy from the corridor.

"Hello, again," I said, blushing.

"May I?" He asked, presenting his arms for dancing.

"You lead," I said, "I've only just learnt this."

"Okay! Hear the beat?" he shouted, squeezing my hand to the rhythm of the song, "One - two? One - two?"

I panicked, bumping my knee into his thigh. His grip tightened as he winced.

"Sorry!" I said, "I'm so sorry!"

"It's alright, darling," he giggled, "Just keep going!"

I carefully bit my lip as we worked. He had pulled me so close that I couldn't see my feet, leaving me no other option but to look him in the face. In my memory, his breath is quick and cool and he's smiling from ear to ear as we bounce up and down together. For strangers under yellow light, we were so, so close.

Before I knew it, he was spinning me under his arm, and as he drew me in close again, he stole a kiss on my cheek.

A cage of little, white butterflies set loose in my belly as we began to waltz. His chest and neck were glistening now and the small, gold charm was sticking to his skin.

"I'm Thomas," he said.

I could have died. We took such outlandish ownership of each other.

"Henry," I said, nodding.

"Nice to meet you, Henry."

"Lovely to meet you, Thomas."

Honestly, I could have died.

"What brings you here?" I asked.

"You remember those boys earlier?" He asked, raising an eyebrow.

"Yes," I said, "…a funny bunch."

"They're usually an absolute scream. Sorry about Taylor, he's not always so rude."

"The one with the moustache?" I asked.

"That's the one," he nodded.

"He wasn't that rude," I said, "I just get nervous. It's not every day you get cornered by three boys."

"Ah, well," he smirked, "He's a nice bloke. His bark's much worse than his bite, so sorry nonetheless. He's determined to find himself a husband, bless him."

"Brave of him. What about the boy on the floor?" I asked.

"We call him Junior," he replied, "His mum caught him reading a certain kind of magazine and he's been out of the house ever since. He lives with us now."

"You live with them as well?" I asked.

"Oh, yes," he said. "I've known them since college."

By now, we had made our way around the floor to some seats in the corner of the room.

"What brings you here?" Thomas asked.

"I'm cat-sitting for my mother," I said. He choked a laugh.

"She's out of town," I explained, "and my father and brother aren't around, so someone had to watch Cookie, but I was bored this evening and felt like going—oh, my God, I wish I could stop talking about my goddam cat!"

I am sure that in that moment all of the blood in my body shot to my face, but it didn't matter. We were laughing and petting each other in that peculiar way men do when they want desperately to touch more—their necks and hands drawn together by some magnificent ghost determined to unite brothers.

We fell silent for a while in our small, red booth and he put his head on my shoulder. His hair smelled sweetly of sweat and something else I couldn't place — it was as if the scent had lifted, looked at my mouth, and kissed my lips, poisoning me with pink clouds, fine china, milky tea, and orange blossoms.

I opened my eyes and found myself kissing him.

"Would you like to come home with me?" I whispered, pressing my cheek against his.

He abruptly sat back, suddenly still, as if he were about to cry, and looked towards the dance floor.

"Yes, I would like that," he said, watching the couples. He sighed, "It's beautiful, isn't it?"

"Beautiful," I said, placing my hand on his knee. He looked back at me and smiled as he did when I had first seen him that evening.

"One last dance?" he asked.

"Do you not want to leave?"

"No, I do," he said, "I just like this. You don't mind, do you?"

"No," I promised, shaking my head, "not at all."

We looked around the room at the red lanterns and the red carpet and the many assorted guests that adorned that blessed old haven for outcasts. The bandleader's arm wrung like a charmed snake, yielding a blissful, final whine from the trombones as we took our positions. There was light applause from the seated guests as the bandleader rapped, "thank-you-thank-you," several times. In the brief silence, a shrill cheer rang out across the room.

"Atta girl, Henry! Atta girl!"

I looked over to find Pamela alone at a table, waving.

Thomas laughed, "She yours?"

"Just a friend…as a matter of fact," I said, "I met her here."

"Amazing the people you run into here, isn't it?"

"Yes," I said, kissing him gently on the mouth. "Absolutely amazing."

The Rain

We stayed at The Golden until closing time. Thomas wanted to stay behind and clear tables — he was head-over-heels in love with the place.

"Thanks for the help, gents," sang Lindsay, who had emerged from behind the curtained entrance, "You can piss off now. Time to go home."

He tottered back through the curtains, muttering, and disappeared.

Thomas giggled, "Funny one, isn't he?"

"He's an absolute dear," I said.

Thomas started for the door, then stopped and turned around.

"I dare you to steal something," he said.

We both exchanged a shrug and looked around the room.

"…What?" I asked.

"Over there," he said, pointing out two abandoned bottles of champagne across the room.

"Come on!" He whispered, making his way to the door.

"What about Lindsay?" I asked.

"He fancies the pants off you, darling, he won't mind."

I was suddenly aware of the sound of my shoes. The first bottle came out of the ice, rumbling and squeaking rather loudly.

Thomas suppressed a laugh, "You'll wake the neighbours!"

"Oh, shut up! You take that one there," I said, nodding to the adjacent bottle. He went to the second table and unearthed the bottle rather impressively.

"Wait, where are we going to hide these?" I asked.

Thomas stroked his chin, "In our shirts?"

"Are you crazy? We won't get out the door with these in —"

Thomas put his hand over my mouth.

"Listen," he whispered, "*bouncers.*"

He put his bottle between his knees and began unbuttoning his shirt. The voices drew nearer.

"Quick, under the table!"

He grabbed my wrist, ducking out of sight. I swung into place beside Thomas, hugging into him trying to stay silent. A pair of black shoes emerged from the swinging door.

I realised that I still had my arm around Thomas and that my hand had landed just below his neck, on his bare chest. He must have unbuttoned his shirt just low enough before he'd dragged me to the floor. The pendant on his necklace was a small, gold rectangle; I could feel his heart beating. I held him quietly as we waited for the men to pass out of sight.

"We ought to go," he whispered, turning to face me.

We froze, gazing at each other's faces, breathing.

He kissed me again, and we sat in each other's arms for a moment longer before slowly untangling ourselves out from underneath the furniture, taking the bottles with us.

We collected our coats.

"Thanks again, gents," Lindsay squawked.

"No, trouble, dear," said Thomas, "See you next week?"

"See you next week," Lindsay nodded.

The head bouncer gurgled a greeting from his stool.

"Goodnight," I said, concealing my champagne under my coat. Thomas was smirking as we stepped outside.

The moment the door shut behind us, we erupted into girlish laughter and made our way to the Strand. The alley way was cold and noisy; the rain had started again, and the entire passage was echoing with the sound of fat drops smacking into standing water. At the entryway back onto the street, Thomas produced his bottle and clinked it against mine. We looked out onto the Strand from the opening of the alley, standing in silence while rain fell.

"Beautiful, isn't it?" I said, grinning over at him.

"Yes," he said, looking at me, "beautiful."

He nudged my elbow and I had to look away from him—I couldn't quite handle his gaze. Taking my arm, he placed his chin on my shoulder.

"Shall we go?" he asked, gently squeezing my bicep, "This champagne isn't going to drink itself."

"I hope not," I winked. "Shall we go?"

We crossed the street.

"I wish the Tube ran all night!" I shouted.

"You would think, wouldn't you, in a city like this!"

We huddled underneath the marquee of the Lyceum Theatre, across the road.

"Why don't we go to mine?" He offered, "You're in Acton — it's ages away! And anyway, I wanted to stay late and now nothing's running and we're stranded and it's completely my fault. It's the least I can do."

I took a big breath of chilled, rainy air.

We watched the puddles ripple and reflect what lights of the streets remained. A few other partygoers were avoiding the downpour, sticking to the sides of buildings like rats in a sewer.

"I do love this city in the rain," I said, stepping out from the marquee to catch a few drops in my mouth.

"What the devil are you doing?" Thomas asked.

"Sobering up," I said, gulping a drop and looking back at him, "you?"

"*Watching* you sober up, I guess. How's it taste?"

"Sobriety, or the rain?" I asked.

"The rain. Don't bother with sobriety, it's terribly old fashioned."

"Fit for a queen," I said, stepping back under the portico. Thomas took my wrist in his hand and checked my watch.

"Three minutes past two."

"Why don't we head to yours?" I asked.

"Okay," he grinned, stepping forward to stick an arm out. He sighed, "Well, at least the champagne will be chilled by the time we get there."

He dropped his arm, looking around for a moment. He looked at me, then up and down the road.

"No cabs, no trains, no buses," he shrugged, crossing himself. "God save the queens!" he declared, as he began to run up the road.

"Wait!" I called out, "We're running?!"

We twisted and turned through streets I'd never seen before, passing empty pubs and splashing through puddles. The rain began to saturate my hair as we reached the flower market, which was covered in old petals and discarded wooden boxes. I scooped up a neglected pink rose that had been left for scrap among the detritus of Saturday afternoon's shoppers and stuffed it into my coat pocket, holding my bottle of champagne with both hands, trying my best to keep it steady as I pounded after Thomas. We were both completely soaked, dizzy, and winded by the time we arrived at his flat in Soho.

"Here, hold this!" he said, stuffing his bottle into my arms while he searched for his keys. He unlocked the door and we piled into the main hall, shoes sopping and coats dripping. As the tight, black door swung to a close, we collapsed into hysterical laughter. I was doubled over against the door as Thomas snickered on the bottom two steps of the building's staircase, eventually propping himself against the bannister.

Our laughter subsided, but our bellies were still hurting. I was unsure if I had rain drops or tears in my eyes. Thomas crawled up the stairs to the landing. I followed slowly, watching him feel his way up the stairs. It looked like his coat had been completely soaked through, and there was quite a bit of dirt at the hem, from where his heels had kicked up mud from the street. Even in his drunken stupor, he was still quite lucid and managed to climb the stairs in a matter of seconds. I admired his bum as he reached the top of the stairs and stood, stretching. To this day, I don't believe for a second that he knew just how attractive he really was.

He greeted his door with a rhythmic knock, and waited. It was marked with small, gold lettering that read *FLAT A,* except the L had fallen off and someone had written two small S's on the end, leaving it to read *FAT Ass.* He groaned impatiently, retrieving his key, and let us into the flat.

We stood in a very small foyer lit by a single bulb in a purple lamp shade. On the floor to my right was a small rack for shoes and above it, at eye level, four empty coat hooks. In the wall to the left hung a small mirror. Just ahead of us lay an archway that served as a passage to the rest of the very small flat.

"Anyone home?" I asked, in a low voice.

"Taylor and Junior met some boys, I think. I don't know."

"Queen's home!" he shouted, shaking his coat off and hanging it on the wall, "Taylor? Junior?" He stepped forward and leaned out, checking through the arch for inhabitants, then turned to me.

"Looks like it's just us," he smiled, "tea?"

"Yes, please," I said, rubbing my hands together.

"Hang your coat up," he nodded, passing out of sight, "Milk and sugar?"

"Just milk, please," I called. I took my shoes off and placed them on the rack. I heard a kettle clatter on the stove as I stepped through the archway into a cozy sitting room large enough to hold an old sofa, an armchair, and a standing lamp. A low coffee table sat in front of the sofa atop a round rug.

There were four doors in the opposite wall: the door to the kitchen, which was closest to me at the right, had been removed. To the left were three closed doors. Thomas popped out of the kitchen.

"Taylor has a few shirts that could fit you. He's the second door there," he said, unbuttoning his silk shirt as he passed through the door on the far left.

"Get out of those wet clothes!" He shouted.

Taylor's room was quite dark and it took me a minute of fumbling around to find the switch to a single, bare bulb that hung from the ceiling. The room smelled of cigarettes and shoe polish and was decorated with the odd photograph and newspaper clipping. I tucked my bowtie into my jacket pocket and began to undress. I selected a knit jumper and swapped my underpants for a pair of Taylor's. My privates were still quite cold and shrunken, and my ego took a bit of a hit at the thought of presenting myself in front of Thomas in my current state. Leaning against the wall, I peeled my socks off, as the kettle started to whistle. My heart leapt a bit, knowing that Thomas would find me in his flatmate's underclothes at any moment. As if by magic, I found a small pair of shorts to wear and had, thankfully, made my way out of sight as Thomas passed by the door.

"You said milk, yeah?" Thomas called from the kitchen.

"Yes, yes," I said, making my way into the sitting room. Thomas was wearing a small pair of blue briefs that clung to his buttocks as if they had been painted directly onto his body, accentuating his obvious athleticism that his formal wear had so devilishly concealed earlier that evening. He had changed into a pair of white socks and a pale-blue button-down shirt, with the sleeves rolled up. Thomas looked up at me and smiled as he stirred some fresh milk into my tea. His hair had dried now, his slicked-back tresses were now tousled blonde locks that were absolutely irresistible.

"Don't be angry," he said, handing me a teacup.

"Why would I be angry?" I asked.

"Taste it. I've slipped a little something into it."

"You haven't drugged me, have you?" I joked. He smiled and shook his head.

"Just a bit of honey," he said, folding his arms, "My mother keeps bees back home."

"That's incredible," I said, tasting the tea, "My complements to the chef."

"Thank you, sir," he said, drawing out the sides of his shirt and curtseying. I smiled and began to move into the sitting room, but something kept me glued to the doorway as he let go of the sides of his shirt and straightened up. He smiled at me, his head slightly wobbling out of what seemed like adoration or attraction. A terrible feeling of worry overcame me as he turned away to prepare his cup.

In that moment, between sweet giggles and soft eyelashes, I could see him with me, in my life, forever.

The Flatmate

"I could kiss you forever," he sighed, smiling softly.

I felt a bit embarrassed and didn't know what to say, so I kissed his fingers instead.

"I've never met anyone like you."

"Well, there's only one me, I suppose," he said, running his fingers over my collarbones, "I've never met anyone like you, either."

"Surely you've met a Henry before?" I asked.

"I've met a few before, but only in passing – and none of any particular note until now." He sat back on my thighs, "Do you like to read, or do you enjoy music at all?"

"I like music a lot. I play the cello, actually, I won a medal at my school's winter concert for cello…and I go to the theatre?"

My stomach began to turn and I shut my eyes.

"Oh," he said, "Do you want to sleep?"

I looked back at him and smiled wearily, "I'm not sleepy, I just feel sort of strange. Sort of dizzy."

He pursed his lips, "Hmm. Maybe finish your tea then see how you feel."

"Good shout," I said, "Where did I put it?"

"I seem to remember things started in the doorway of the kitchen?" He suggested.

We had arrived at the flat and lost ourselves in each other's arms, neglecting our tea. I located mine on the small table in the sitting room. I could still taste the honey. He followed me to his door.

"Gone cold, has it?" He smirked, "I suppose we found a bit of heat elsewhere." He leaned against his doorframe, peeling off his socks.

"Yes, sir," I nodded, sipping at my tea, "did you find yours?"

"No luck, yet," he said, bouncing back into his room.

"Where do you find your shirts, by the way? I especially liked that silk one you had on earlier," I said, leaning against his doorway to watch him search.

"Oh, Selfridge's, I think — or it was a Christmas gift — can't remember!" He said, turning in circles, "Where the hell did I put it?"

"There it is," I pointed, spotting it under the bed.

"How the hell did it end up there?" He asked, getting down on his belly to reach for his cup. I enjoyed the view of his backside.

"What time is it?" I asked.

"It is now…" he said, standıng to check the small clock by his bed, "nearly a quarter to four."

"I'm not tired, actually. Isn't that bizarre?"

"Not really, we're having a nice time," he said, sitting on his bed and sipping his tea, "I'm a bit hungry actually. What about you?"

I considered this, realising I hadn't had a bite to eat since I left my flat for the ballroom. I suddenly became very aware of the void in my belly and nodded, "I am, actually."

"Can I cook for you?"

This young man sat before me on his messy bed, nested in a whirlpool of striped sheets, and I wanted nothing more than to go to him and cling to him tightly. I was a bit speechless – we'd so quickly connected in a way that seemed too good to be true. He was sensitive and smart and sexy. It was easy. So spectacularly easy.

"Absolutely."

"What do you fancy?" He asked, bounding to the door.

"Anything. I just need a bit to take the edge off," I said, curling up in the bed.

"I'm not sure what I have. We might need to do something simple this time," he said, heading into the kitchen, "Let me have a gander."

I heard him open and shut a few cupboards.

He called back, "Toast, maybe? …with Marmite?"

"Sounds perfect," I said.

I shut my eyes.

***

I was awakened by a small splash of water on my face. The curtains had been drawn and Thomas's only window was wide open, filling the room with the morning's soft, grey light. The rain had carried on through the night and had pooled on the windowsill, occasionally flicking lighter drops through the window onto my face. I was still wearing my borrowed jumper and shorts, but my borrowed socks had been removed, carefully folded, and placed on the bedside table. Alone, I let out one of those glorious, early morning sighs that singlehandedly greet, curse, and begin the day, stretching long-ways and twisting myself back into the comfort of the sheets, hoping to find a trace of that marvellous smell that had followed Thomas around the previous evening. A breeze crept in, chilling me, and I landed my bare feet on the cold, wood floor and crept to the door, remembering that all of my clothing was in Taylor's room. I pulled the door open a few inches to find the sitting room empty, and my clothing carefully spread out over the sofas – I could smell coffee.

"Thomas?" I called, lowly. I heard a chair shuffle away from a table in the kitchen.

"She lives!" Thomas shouted, "Come join me, darling!"

I waddled to the doorway of the kitchen to find Thomas sat at a small table, with the kitchen's only window open as wide as it could go.

"I love mornings like this," Thomas said, "I love the rain so much! And I like how outside smell mixes with cooking and coffee smell, do you know what I mean?"

I rubbed my eyes.

"Coffee?" He asked.

"Yes, please," I said, "What the hell happened?"

"I would like to ask you the same question — you didn't eat anything at the ballroom, did you? If you did, you should have known better. The food there is horrific."

"No, no. I had breakfast and I ate before I left for the club," I said, taking my place at the table.

The sunlight was pouring into the kitchen and his face seemed to be glowing, the little speckles in his bright blue eyes like sea foam on waves of blue and blue and more blue.

"Well, what time was that?" He asked, raising an eyebrow.

"Must have been around six? Seven?" I said.

"There we are, then. We were up until about four. That's…what?" He counted on his fingers, nibbling at his bottom lip. He was beautiful in the day time as well.

"That's ten hours, Henry. Ten hours without food and you were drinking lots. Of course you passed out."

"That would explain it, wouldn't it?" I blushed, "I don't normally do that. I guess I just lost track. Time flies?"

"Time flies, but you still should have eaten something. You're lucky you weren't stumbling back to Acton in the dark. Could have been bad," he said, shaking his finger playfully at me. I felt bad for imposing.

"I'm so sorry," I said, "I wasn't sick, was I?"

"No, not at all. Don't be sorry. You're very handsome when you sleep, by the way. I was terribly sad you were out cold so soon. I suppose it's best we behaved ourselves," he said, cracking a smile into his coffee cup.

He rose and found another cup and saucer for me in the cupboard by the stovetop. He stole a glance at me as he picked up the coffee pot. Everything about him smiled — his eyes, his cheeks, even his hands.

"Did we…" I started.

He shook his head, "No, I slept in Junior's room. I didn't want you to think…well, you know."

"Please tell me you didn't eat toast alone."

"I didn't, I prefer your company," he smiled.

He offered the coffee, our fingers touching as I took the cup and saucer. They hardly made contact, really, but it was enough to make my heart jump, so I brought my other hand swiftly to the rescue, setting the coffee down on the table. Thomas produced a carton of cigarettes from his shirt pocket. I watched him finger one out and pop it between his lips.

"Want one?"

I nodded.

He tugged a second cigarette from the carton and presented the filter end in front of my lips. I took it in my mouth, blushing as he produced a small matchbox from the same pocket, and he lit it. I choked on the smoke for a moment, but gallantly recovered, however, I suddenly felt as if I had never smoked a single cigarette in my entire life. He lit his own with another match, flicking it out the window once it had been extinguished. Though we were still quiet, we both understood we were headed for uncharted territory, like soldiers entering into war. We shared a lack of knowledge of what was to come, and we shared the subsequent, mutual fear of that unknown.

I noticed a small houseplant behind him, atop the refrigerator.

"That's nice," I said, "where'd you get it?"

He turned around, following my pointed finger, and took a drag on his cigarette.

"Not mine," he said. "It's Taylor's. He likes plants, or at least he says he does. It's only a money tree. If you spit in its general direction once a month, it sticks it out rather well."

There was the sound of a key in the front door. Thomas leaned to the side, to watch the door from his seat.

"Who calls?" he shouted.

A voice replied back, "Janet Gaynor, *cunt*!"

Thomas replied as Garbo, "Want to be alone, darling?"

"Yes, very much so. I got stuck with the most awful drag last night," the voice carried on from the other room, "Hung like a race horse, but couldn't speak a word of English. I couldn't tell if he was asking for directions or talking dirty to me. We're in *England*, for God's sake, why doesn't anyone speak any *bloody English?!*"

Taylor barrelled into the kitchen, finding himself silent at the sight of a visitor in his kitchen. His brown overcoat was worn around the buttonholes. He hadn't changed clothing since I'd seen him the previous evening.

"Oh. Hello," he said curtly, his moustache twitching at the sight of me. His eyes darted to Thomas. I looked at Thomas, a bit embarrassed.

"You must be?" He droned.

Thomas cleared his throat, "Taylor, this is Henry."

Taylor looked shocked.

"Ooh! He has a name this time! Unlike you to learn names, isn't it?"

Thomas took another drag on his cigarette as Taylor presented his hand — as if he were expecting a small kiss on the back of it.

"Henry," I said, extending a hand.

Taylor turned to Thomas, "And did you sleep in my bed last night?"

"Yes," said Thomas, "Henry wasn't feeling well, so I jumped into yours. Hope you don't mind."

"Yeah, fine," he said, shooting his words between the two of us and out the window. I felt like calling a cease-fire.

"I should be going," I said. Thomas's face fell.

"You haven't finished your coffee," he protested.

"I know, but I don't want to impose, really, and I ought to grab a bite to eat. And the cat, of course," I said.

Taylor interjected, "Nothing worse than an angry pussy."

"I'll just hop out of these clothes," I said, "I'm more than happy to take them home and wash them for you."

I began to head out of the kitchen to collect my suit.

"Don't worry about it, I can wash them," assured Thomas, who had pushed by Taylor to follow me, "Are you sure you have to go right now?"

I glanced over Thomas's shoulder into the kitchen. Taylor was rinsing out my cup in the sink. I took Thomas by the hand.

"Help me get changed?" I asked. Thomas smiled brightly and grabbed my suit.

"I think your socks are in here," he said, heading into his bedroom. Thomas shut the door behind us and tossed my suit on the bed.

"Don't worry about Taylor — he's harmless. I think he's just a bit jealous. When we saw you in the corridor last night he practically died on the spot. Fancies the pants off you."

While he spoke I had slipped Taylor's jumper off and sat on the bed. Thomas was straddling me, his bare legs and those perfect blue briefs settling in close. We kissed slowly.

"I wish you didn't have to leave," he said.

"I wish I could stay, but I really should get home. What good is a secret affair if I give myself away from the beginning by accidentally starving the cat to death?"

He dismounted and sat next to me on the bed.

"Fair enough," he said, "I'm sorry about him."

"Don't be," I said, "Help me with my shirt."

I stood up and fed my arms through the sleeves of my shirt, standing in front of Thomas, who was on his knees, on the bed. I placed my hands on his hips and let him button his way up my chest. The butterflies stirred.

"Can I see you again?" I asked quietly. He smiled, taking one of my hands to fasten my cuffs. He buttoned the sleeve and kissed my hand.

"I'd like that very much," he said, repeating the same gesture on my other cuff. I held his face in my hands. He had lovely little ears that sprung back into place with such life if you twiddled with them. He kissed me, then pulled away from me, looking at my waist.

"Taylor will want his shorts back," he said, smiling.

"You smile an awful lot," I said.

"I smile when I'm happy," he said, "Now get out of those shorts."

The Phone Call

I made my way through Soho in the rain, passing the sex shops and darkened neon lights. Two broad-shouldered, hairy-legged ladies stumbled out of the Gargoyle Club. Between the two costume-shop dresses slumped a thin gentleman with a great deal of red about his mouth. A long bandage dangled out from underneath his shirt, which dragged the ground as he was shovelled into a black cab. I bought two apples from a street vendor and hopped the Tube home.

I thought of Thomas as I left the train and as I walked to my flat, passing the large estate near the station. I thought of his arms as I wiped my feet at my doorstep, and I thought of his tongue as I slid the key into the door.

Cookie, our cat, seemed pleased to see me. She was curled up in a smoky, grey ball of fur and greeted me from atop our sofa. I searched for my billfold and discovered the pink rose I had picked up in Covent Garden while sprinting through the rain. I kissed it lightly, its fresh dew smelling sweetly of a London night. I went up our carpeted, boxy staircase and walked along the landing to my childhood bedroom. It was much too small for me now, but I had managed to elevate the room's décor to a level of sophistication that numbed that dreadful feeling that comes with being back at home after tasting freedom. I got undressed and ran a bath. As I checked the water, I remembered to feed Cookie. I scampered downstairs stark-naked through our sitting room and into the kitchen.

"Come on, Cooks," I chirped. She rolled off the sofa and followed me into the kitchen.

"Where the hell have you been?" she seemed to say, "Another late night?"

"Don't give me that look," I said, "Sorry, I'm so late."

I opened a tin of cat food and emptied it into her bowl by our sliding glass door. She moseyed through my legs, tickling the back of my knee with her tail. She crouched and began to eat. I left her in peace to go watch the bath. I fetched the rose from my room and leaned against the sink as the water filled the tub. I pulled the rose apart, dropping petals in the bath as the water gushed from the tap. I slid into the tub and stewed, my legs aching from the night before. A few petals collected on top of my chest, like little boats docking in a hairy harbour, and I dreamed more of Thomas. I had left my telephone number with him that morning and was hoping for a call. I couldn't wait to hear his voice again. After half an hour or so, I pulled the drain and let the water out, staying in the tub as my liquid blanket pulled away from my skin and the petals settled along my body. The air began to chill me. I got out of the tub and peeled the petals off, then dried and dressed. I remembered how hungry I was and thought of what we might have left over in the cupboard downstairs.

Cookie was birdwatching from one of our large windows. She liked to sit among the little china dolls my mother collected and displayed on a small table that was covered by a knitted runner she had made a few Christmases ago. Our flat was a funny amalgamation of pinks, reds, browns, and beiges; with hints of yellow pastel appearing throughout. The sitting room of our semi-detached house had two pink sofas and two large windows at either side of a thin fireplace. Under one window was a low bookcase and under the other was the table where Cookie was sitting. The walls were decorated with a few paintings my brother had made several years ago when he was at school. He was in the army now and we hadn't heard from him in a very long time.

The kitchen was outfitted in yellowed linoleum flooring, and the cupboards were all a dark, stained wood with black, die-cast handles. In lieu of a kitchen island stood a large butcher's block that my grandfather had made by hand. It was a gift to my parents on their wedding day. Since the divorce, however, its charm had fallen silent and it was subsequently never used. Father had been a stickler for keeping things pristine, a sentiment that was all too consuming for my taste. A few of my mother's cross-stitch animal portraits hung on the wall in little oval frames above a dining table that was squeezed tightly into the corner by our sliding door. I peeked into the cupboards, on the hunt for food. We didn't have much, so I scrambled some eggs and had them over toast. I ate quickly and was still hungry, so I opened a tin of chicken soup and put it a saucepan to warm. While I waited, I went to check up on Cookie.

"Anything interesting, my dear?" I asked, scratching behind her ears.

She didn't reply. I looked at the clock – a little porcelain figurine of two cherubs embracing: Mother was due back in a few hours.

My soup began to bubble. I switched the hob off and transferred the contents of the pot into my father's left-behind crockery. It had been a gift from his mother — more beige with odd blue and yellow flowers beneath a large rooster. My brother always thought they were charming. I didn't care for the design, but I liked how large the bowls were, so I took advantage of them. I saluted my brother, wherever he was, as I went to the sitting room to eat — a ritual I only allowed myself when Mother was away. I sat on the floor, with my back against the sofa. Cookie came to join me, perching behind my head. Occasionally, between bites, I would drop my head backward to rest it on the sofa. Cookie, who would lie just so that the bend in my neck would allow her room to breathe, would then lick at my ears. Thomas and I never did open that champagne.

Despite having chronic bouts of loneliness, there was nothing like having the house to myself. I had just finished my soup, letting Cookie clean out the little amount of broth that was left in the bottom of the bowl, when the telephone rang. My heart pounded as I lifted the receiver.

"Hello?"

"Hello, pet! It's Pamela! Tell us everything!"

My heart sank.

"Hi, Pamela, I'm alright, thank you."

"Oh, darling, you're too funny! So, how was the blonde?"

I considered telling her about the dancing and the drinking and talking and the kissing; about the champagne and the encounter under the table and his bouncing, blue briefs.

"Tell me, dear, who were *you* with?"

"You mean *Anton*?"

"I guess? I don't know who he is, Pamela. I didn't even see you with anyone!" I looked at the clock again.

"He told me he works for the *government*," she said, "he's one of the most honest men I've ever met, if you must know," she said, close to tears, by the sound of it.

"Listen, Pam, I've got to go. Next time I see you, I'd love to meet him, if you'd like. I have to go. Ta, ta," I began to replace the receiver, but something turned in me and I heard myself say, "Oh, by the way, his name is Thomas and I went back to his place last night. I'm seeing him again later this week."

I slammed the receiver down. I felt my head go a bit fuzzy. Cookie came over to me.

"She's horrendous," she meowed.

"I know, Cooks," I sighed, "I know."

***

The Phone Call

I had fallen asleep on the sofa with Cookie atop my chest when the doorbell woke me up. Two rings were followed by a few raps at the base of the door. Mother was home. I opened the door, a bit dazed.

"Was there a duck in your closet last night?" She laughed.

"Hello, mother," I sighed as she shoved two brown grocery bags into my arms.

"Hello, darling, thank you, yes," she said, kissing my forehead, "Cookie okay?"

She sailed into the house.

"And I'm fine, thanks," I said, "Cooks and I have been napping."

"Hence the bedhead?" She prompted, heading into the sitting room.

"Hence the bedhead," I repeated.

"What did you do yesterday? I came by to drop off some stuff from the office and you weren't here. Come help me put these away," she said, dropping her handbag on the sofa as she sailed into the kitchen, summoning me with a single outstretched (and polished) finger.

"Oh, I went into town. Felt like a walk," I diverted, following her into the kitchen.

"Went into town for a walk. That's peculiar," she spoke as she began to open the cupboards. I placed the bags on the butcher's block.

"Careful with that one," she said, shaking a hand at the bag in my right arm, "that idiot bag boy put my eggs somewhere near the bottom. Honestly, they throw your groceries around in this country as if they were rocks."

We began to put the food away, the odd bits into the ice box. I was in the middle of situating a box of pasta at the back of the cupboard when a metallic sound came from the sitting room. Cookie had returned to my leftovers and had nudged the spoon around in the bowl.

"Henry," my mother sparked, "what have I told you about eating in there?"

"I didn't get it on anything, it's fine."

"Well, someday when you spill tomato soup and grease on our sofas, we'll have a very different conversation."

"I look forward to it. I might burn the house down while I'm at it," I smirked, "How's your week been?"

"Very good, thank you. It's been pretty hectic. The girls and I were beside ourselves to be out of the city for a bit. Wales was lovely, but I much preferred our little room they got for us in town for the last two days. The convention went really smoothly, so the boys were happy with that. It's nice when they're happy. When they're in a mood, they can be quite nasty, especially to poor Beatrice."

"Is that the temp they got recently?" I asked, retrieving the bowl and spoon from the sitting room. I gave Cookie a quick scratch under the chin.

"Yes," she said, moving the eggs from the carton into the fridge, "She's only been with us a few weeks. Very green, but she's sweet. We all get on well."

"That's nice," I said, washing up my bowl and spoon. She spoke for about a minute more, but I had lost myself, thinking about Thomas. I put the dishes to the side to dry.

"I will admit," she added, "She is from Blackpool and I can't understand a single word she says."

"I might go up to my room for a bit," I said, pretending to yawn. Mother looked as if she'd been slapped.

"I just got back," she moaned, "Not even a cup of tea?"

"No, really," I fibbed, "I'm kind of beat. I had a lot to eat earlier and I'm just in one of those sleepy moods."

"You boys are funny," she said, "Well, alright, sweetie." She came forward to kiss my forehead once more, "See you in a bit. Don't sleep too long, you'll ruin your week."

I smiled, "Yes, ma'am."

Cookie followed me up to my bedroom. I wondered if Thomas was ever going to call me. It had been such an incredible few hours spent with him and I could hardly bear the thought of our first encounter being our last. As I fell in and out of sleep, I would wake up and find Cookie snuggled close, other times, she was nowhere to be found. Now that Mother was home, there wasn't any chance Thomas would be coming to the house unless she went away again. His touch was such brief magic, and I ached at the thought of our distance. I recalled the silk shirt and the glow of my match in his eyes. I called back the taste of champagne on his lips and the way his chest felt under the table. I had just slipped my hands down the front of my pants when I heard the phone ring downstairs.

47

The Visit

Before I could get to the phone, I heard my mother pick up the receiver. While Cookie zipped down the steps to watch, I stayed out of sight at the top of the landing.

"Hello?" My mother's voice lilted, "Yes, he does…Is something wrong? …Oh, well, that's very sweet of you… Yes, he's just upstairs." She called out, "Henry? There's a Mr. Sanders on the phone."

I didn't know a Mr. Sanders. I bobbed down the stairs and took the receiver from her briskly.

"He says he was in the year below you at school," she whispered, "he remembers your cello performance at the winter concert and he wants you to give him lessons!"

"Really? In the year below me?" I asked, raising an eyebrow. I spoke into the receiver, hoping mother would clear off, but she wouldn't budge.

"Hello?"

A musical salutation scampered down the line and into my ears, striking me directly through the heart.

"Hello, handsome."

My stomach leapt.

"Thomas?" I gasped, my face flushing. I quickly recovered, "Thomas *Sanders*?"

"I was wondering if you could help me with something," he said, "are you busy later this week? I was hoping we might be able to arrange…a cello lesson or two?"

I could *feel* him smiling down the phone. Mother stood happily with her arms folded, beaming that her son was *practically* a *celebrity*. I tried to keep from blushing as Thomas continued.

"I thought we made some pretty wonderful music together…It would be a shame to leave such a beautiful thing unfinished, wouldn't it?"

My mother put her hand over my forehead.

"Darling," she whispered, "are you alright?"

"I'm fine, Mother," I hissed, returning to the phone, "I'm free Thursday, are you?

Mother put her hands on her hips as I tried to keep my hand from shaking. Thomas spoke in a lower tone.

"The boys don't leave the flat until three. Would that be alright?"

"Yes, yes," I said, keeping up the charade, "Thursday at three sounds excellent."

"There's a shop on Dean Street."

"I'd love to. I'll see you Thursday. Thanks for calling, Mr. Sanders."

I hung up the receiver. Mother frowned.

"Darling," she huffed, "You said you would help me with the tea on Thursday!"

"I know," I sighed, "but it seems an awfully rude thing to decline his offer. He seems like a really respectful boy."

"Well, I suppose I can manage," she spat, "but don't run out on me again, young man. Cucumber sandwiches and lemon squares are difficult to manage by yourself. You're lucky you're my favourite son."

"That I am," I said, kissing her on the cheek.

"I'm glad that you're making some money at least," she sighed. "You can't live off the old allowance forever. It's so sweet of an underclassman to reach out to a senior boy — he must be a very big fan."

"He must be," I chuckled, "perhaps he is."

Mother hugged me and headed back into the kitchen. Cookie and I exchanged glances.

"Thursday at three," I whispered, "I'm seeing him on Thursday at three."

I could have burst into song or burst into tears as I ran up to my room, counting days and hours and seconds until I could see him and smell him and touch him and talk with him. I wondered what we might get up to; where we'd go. My heart was singing. I could sleep soundly knowing I could see my Thomas in a mere two days…however, Wednesday dragged along endlessly. I had hardly finished my boiled eggs that morning when the doorbell rang. Mother put down her cross-stitch and answered the door. Upon hearing my mother squeal, "Pamela! Darling!" I crossed my fingers and hoped for death.

"However are you, my dear? So lovely to see you!"

There was more squealing followed by a sound that made my privates run for cover.

Pamela said, "Is Henry in? I *must* speak to him!"

"Yes, of course, he's here!" Mother said, calling for me, "Henry! There's someone here to see you!"

It was in a moment of surprising charity that I had struck up a conversation with Pam at The Golden, under the influence of several gin and gingers. Her dress was particularly striking under the red lights, and it was her overloaded wrists and fingers that had caught my eye in the first place.

"Your ring is lovely!" I shouted over the music. Pamela turned her head towards me, her eyes inflating immediately.

"Oh, thank you, petal! This one is from India, this one is from Paris, and this one is from Bond Street!" She cackled.

"You've been to India?"

"Oh, no, pet, but I met a Maharaja at The Ritz once! The ring *itself* is from India. Wouldn't dare go there nowadays. Absolutely *ghastly!*"

"I take it Paris is all too abhorrent as well, then?" I laughed.

"Non, non, mon petit garçon," she fluttered, "*J'adore Paris!*"

Her accent was atrocious and so was her breath, however, something about her amused me. I thought she might make an interesting companion. Little did I know when I enlisted with Pamela that she would be on my doorstep some time later speaking to my mother, who absolutely adored her. Needless to say, we never told her how or where we'd met considering I, in my drunken stupor, had also informed

Pamela about my more nefarious adventures around town with *men*. As far as Mother was concerned, I met Pamela while working during the summer – which was a boldface lie. At times, I was genuinely surprised how easily Mother was fooled by our stories. Pamela scratched her small heels on the mat in the foyer and took off her large coat.

"Henry, Henry, Henry!" She pranced over to me in the kitchen. Her jet black hair had been lopped off into a small, black bob with tiny finger-curls gelled tightly to her face.

"Pamela! I see you've got your locks chopped!" I said, kissing her quickly on the cheek.

"I know! Isn't it the most? Toss your cares and curls away, as they say!"

"I didn't know they were saying that! Looks divine, dear."

"What have you been up to, then?" I asked, "Shall I put the kettle on?"

"Oh, please!"

"Very good," I said, leaping at the opportunity to move away from her. I filled our little red kettle to the brim and sparked up the hob. I leaned against the butcher's block and invited her to sit down at the table.

"Right," I asked, "How are things?"

She tugged at her small black gloves as she worked through a series of broken beginnings, trying to find a place to start. With her left hand finally bare, she suddenly found a groove and began to speak fluidly, unloading the burdens of the past twenty-four hours since we'd last spoke over the phone. She was wearing a long-sleeved day dress that stopped just below the knees. It was mint green with a ruffled neckline that plunged so dangerously close to her breasts that it became impeccably apparent, from where I standing, that she was quite top-heavy. She pulled a cigarette from a small, silver case and clicked over to the hob next to me, lighting her cigarette from the flame under the kettle before finally leaning against the sliding glass door opposite me.

"And then, right before he left, he told me that he never worked in the government after all! I just can't take any more dishonesty, Henry, I just can't take it, pet! All these men masquerading and telling me this and telling me that, and I just can't tell the forest for the trees, or whatever the saying is. Men are beasts!"

"I think that's correct, yes," I said.

"They are, aren't they?" She wept.

"No, no, I meant the saying, 'forest for the trees,' is correct," I replied.

"Oh, yes. Right," she said, puffing away.

Mother sang out from the other room, "I smell smo-o-oke!"

I reached over Pamela's shoulder to open the sliding door a few inches.

"Mother doesn't really like smoke in the house…except when she's here alone…then she *loves* it," I joked. Pamela cracked a small smile and wiped a single tear from her eye. I did feel a bit bad for her.

"Oh, come here, old girl," I said, opening my arms.

She folded her free hand around me and tilted her head so her makeup wouldn't smudge. At a distance, we might have resembled two penguins necking. She wrapped her cigarette-wielding hand around my neck and took a drag, my nose nearly missing a scald as she exhaled through the crack in the sliding door. We moved apart.

"Anyway," she sniffled, "how are you? What about that boy you mentioned?"

She sat down at the dining table. My stomach dropped as I realised my mother was still in the next room, quietly cross-stitching.

"What boy?" I said, making a 'cut-throat' motion to her. She very quickly understood.

"Oh, oh, sorry. I meant…" her voice faded as she searched for an alternate word to cover her tracks. The kettle began to scream.

I shouted over the steam, "I've always wanted to go to the *Savoy*, yes!"

She silently mouthed an apology and I waved the misstep away to prepare the tea.

"Can you keep an eye on the time for us? We need to steep about four minutes."

"No trouble," she said, checking her watch. She counted the little tick marks and made a very obvious mental note. I was always conflicted over Pamela, but in the end her idiosyncrasies were just enough to make me absolutely mad for her. I remembered that Thomas would be in my arms the very next day.

"You seem very smiley," she said, pointedly, "Something up, Hen?"

Her cigarette was burning so heavily that the ash was almost hanging by a single thread of tobacco. I jumped up to retrieve the ashtray from the sitting room. Mother and Cookie were occupying the two sofas.

"Everything alright, sweetie?" Mother asked, keeping her eyes on her needlework.

"Yes, just fine," I said, looking around the room, "Have you seen the ashtray?"

"Under the window, I think. I moved it earlier because Miss Cookie was being rather naughty near it. I was worried she was going to knock it off the shelf."

"Thanks," I said, weaving between the sofas. I removed it from the shelf and trailed my fingers along the top of the cushion in hopes of engaging Cookie in a quick game of chase. She was otherwise occupied with the tassels on one of the large pillows. As I petted Cookie, Mother whistled a little.

"You're very popular today," Mother said.

"Not as popular as old Cooks, am I?" I deflected.

Cookie meowed as if to say, "Go back to your guest, dear, and leave me to ravage this pillowcase."

She dug her claws into the arm of the sofa and watched me return to the kitchen.

"Here you are, P," I said, placing the ashtray on the table.

"Thank you so much," she said, "We've got about a minute left."

I sighed. I decided there and then that I hated waiting and I hated time and I hated having to wait to see Thomas again. I hated that I had to wait for tomorrow and then wait some more until three in the afternoon.

We eventually poured the tea and stole a few biscuits from Mother's secret stash of custard creams. Pamela wasn't all bad, and after a few hours she decided to head back to her flat in Holland Park. She invited me to come to dinner that weekend.

"Perhaps our *place,"* she said, winking at me in the foyer.

"Perhaps, Pamela, perhaps," I said, "Get home safe. It's lovely to see you."

"Bye, bye, petal. I'll see you when I see you!"

I closed the door behind her, thanking God Pamela had provided a not altogether unpleasant distraction for a few slim hours.

The Café

Shaftesbury Avenue was bustling with bookshops and businessmen. I was very, very early for my date with Thomas and was practically crippled with nerves as I crossed over Dean Street. I decided to head toward the Palace and hang a left. Soho was quiet, and I passed a cafe that looked like the perfect place to kill a few minutes. Ducking in through the chocolate brown door, I ordered a black coffee and snagged a small table. I debated selecting a cake, but I was already jittery enough and a chocolate spill or a strawberry stain was the last thing I needed. I was trying to focus on an article in a left-behind Evening Standard when an older, bald woman, impeccably dressed in a faux fur coat and diamond earrings, entered. Her bright orange ascot gave some of the assorted baked goods in the window particular competition for most vibrant colours, and her black high-heels reflected the sun sharply as she floated in, ordered, and sat at the table beside me. The sun was filling the cafe with hot gold light and I lit a cigarette, watching my smoke curl and billow up to the painted ceiling. I felt the eyes of the adjacent queen look me over. I glanced to my left and our eyes met.

"Afternoon," she squawked, smiling tightly. Her smoky eyes and pink cheeks gave the impression of a drag queen off the clock. She looked good for her age, though her age was rather apparent; despite this, she seemed to glow somewhat magnificently to me.

"Afternoon," I said, politely. I never knew if I was being eyed by a predator or an ally in these situations. Nevertheless, I enjoyed the attention and was glad to find that my best suit was doing me favours. The waitress, a short, mannish woman in her fifties, shuffled over and set my coffee down in front of me.

"She's like something out of a magazine," the queen remarked, referring to the waitress.

"Like what?" I gulped.

"The staple," she said, pausing briefly before letting a cackle rattle out of her throat.

I giggled, sipping my coffee and burning my top lip. I jerked my face back suddenly and spilled a few drops on the table top and the saucer.

"A bit hot," I shrugged. The bald vulture cackled some more.

"I'm Abbey," she said, extending a decorated hand, "I don't go for the kids, love, so easy does it, nothing to fear."

Her nails were robin-egg blue and she wore three gold rings across her shaved fingers.

"Henry," I said, shaking the hand.

"Would you like a little nappy?"

"A what?"

"A napkin, for your spillage. You'll be thrown out of the place in seconds."

"Oh, that. Yes, I can—"

Before I could finish, Abbey was up and trotting to the counter. The waitress growled.

"Imagine that," Abbey quipped, "Lady Macbeth stuck in a café! Tragic, really!"

She waltzed back over to me, waving a serviette above her head.

"Mind if I sits?" she asked, clicking a nail on the top of the chair opposite me.

"No, not at all," I said.

"Ta."

Abbey let her coat slip off and hung it on the back of the chair. She was wearing a black jumpsuit, decorated with bright green herons and an oriental pattern.

"What brings you here?"

She asked, placing her elbows on the table and clasping her hands by her face. I took a drag on my cigarette, which must have reminded her of her own stash. She promptly produced one of her own and borrowed my lighter.

"I'm waiting for someone," I said.

She gave me a knowing nod, "Ooo! A date?"

"Yes, sort of," I said, shifting in my seat.

Abbey suddenly seemed excited, "Is he coming here?"

"No," I assured, "I'm meeting him on Dean Street. I'm just a bit early."

"Don't want to seem too eager, do we? Smart, that."

"Exactly," I said, blushing.

"Oh, he's gone all red," she pouted, "Do you like him, then? Tickle you pink, does he?"

"You could say that, yes," I said. The queen put both of his hands over his heart and sighed.

"I remember my Freddie. Such a long time ago now, it was practically the stone ages. It was tough in those days with no telephones. You had to make your arrangements in person. You'd leave a place and hope neither of you were too drunk to forget."

I suddenly felt that I had made a friend.

"Did it ever go wrong?" I asked.

"Oh, did it ever go wrong, he asks. Of course, my little flower, it went wrong. I've had my fair share of stand-ups," she said, smoking.

Then she grinned, "And a couple of bend-overs and kneel-downs, for that matter."

I laughed a little too loud and the swarthy waitress scowled at us from behind her till. Abbey's laugh was quite high and wiry. I tried to cool my coffee with a few short breaths across the top of it.

"Have you lived in London long?" I asked.

"I've lived long, but not in London. Bolton, mostly," she winced, "Not nice. I like it here much better." She puffed on her cigarette, "What time you meeting this boy, then?"

"Three," I said, sipping at my coffee. Lady Macbeth tottered over and smacked down a teacup in front of Abbey.

"Oh, that's soon, isn't it? You nervous?"

"Nervous, but excited, yes," I said.

"Don't worry yourself, petal, I'll be here. I'm always here, love. You're a sweet boy, Henry. Who's the lucky fellow?"

"His name is Thomas," I beamed.

"Good name!" She interjected, pointing at me with her cigarette.

I shrugged, "And…? I met him a few nights ago in town, and we got along rather well."

"Did you get on?"

"No, no. We didn't. I passed out."

"Was it that big, darling?"

Abbey threw her head back laughing and smacked the table with her bejewelled hand. I blushed.

"Well," I continued, "I live at my mother's. I ate before I left, but by the time I got into town and after several cigarettes and drinks…I lost track of time. It's easy to lose track of time with him."

"Sounds dreamy," she pecked, "sounds blonde."

"He is, actually!" I said.

"Well dressed? Terribly dreamy with great big blue eyes?"

"Yes," I gushed.

"Even better," she replied, "Sounds like my Freddie."

"Where did you meet Freddie?"

"It's an old club over by Waterloo Bridge. I haven't been since we were kids," she said, smoking. She looked around, but there weren't any ashtrays on the nearby tables.

Abbey gestured to the saucer underneath my coffee cup.

"May I?"

"Oh, of course," I said. She rubbed the ash off of the tip of the cigarette, careful to avoid the cup.

"Ta," she winked.

"Do you have the time?" I asked.

She checked her dainty, silver watch, "You best be off, love. It's nearly ten to three!"

I slurped my coffee down, placing the cup on the table.

"Gosh, I'm almost late," I said.

"Better almost late than late, darling!" She said, scooting her chair away from the table and standing. I shuffled out between the tables.

"Thanks for the chat, Abbey," I said, presenting my hand, "Perhaps I'll see you around."

"Between you and me, it's *Arthur,* but all my friends call me Abbey," he smiled, "Wait! Take this," he said, producing a small conker from his pocket and folding it into my hand, "I found this in Green Park earlier this morning and was wondering if I should keep it or not. I think you might like a little good luck with your man. Take it."

"Thank you, Abbey," I said, pocketing the conker, "Thank you very much."

"Now, go see your boy! Love him fiercely. There is no other love but fierce love. Otherwise, it's just a waste! Now, go!"

Abbey patted me on the shoulder. I smiled and turned to go, opening the door.

The waitress shouted, "You haven't paid me!"

Abbey waved me on, "Get going, pet. My treat!"

"Thank you so much!" I said, frantically blowing out the door and picking up my pace down the street towards Soho. My shoes were not made to run in, but I was getting on as best I could. I passed by the Palace again, under the marquee for *No, No, Nanette,* and turned right onto Dean Street. I stopped myself to catch my breath and began to walk again, shaking uncontrollably. I wondered if I would find his flat again easily or if he would be waiting for me on a street corner, perhaps on his doorstep. I continued to search for door numbers, all of which meant nothing to me until, in a single moment of petrifying realisation, I remembered that I did not know Thomas' address, his phone number, his real surname, or anything about him that would allow me to find him ever again. There wasn't even a music shop – it had all been lies!

I produced the conker I had received moments before, knowing Abbey was probably back at the cafe feeling quite proud of her action of charity and consideration for the younger generation, and looked at it.

I held it to my forehead and began to cry.

The Meeting

I heard a voice behind me.

"Henry?"

I turned around, trying to dry my eyes. It was him.

"Oh, my god," I gasped, trying to hold myself together, "Hello, you."

"Hello," he said, almost whispering, "I was worried for a minute you wouldn't show up. I remembered after we spoke on the telephone that I hadn't told you where to meet me."

I put the conker back in my pocket and hugged him. He smelled exactly the same and his ear felt so lovely against the side of my face. I sneaked a small kiss on his cheek. He grinned as we came apart.

"It's awfully nice to see you," I said.

"Sorry, I'm a bit late," he said, "I had to do a few turns up and down the street to find you. I knew you'd be here, I just knew it, but I didn't know where you'd end up. I'm so sorry if I worried you."

I couldn't find the words to respond, so I said, "I met a drag queen in a cafe around the corner and he gave me this," pulling the conker back out of my pocket. "She wished me luck today," I said, struggling to catch my breath, "I'm so glad to see you."

"Not every day you get a present from a drag queen, is it?"

"No," I laughed, "No, it's not."

We both stood on the pavement, looking at each other.

"Well," said Thomas, "shall we?"

"Yes, let's," I said, putting my hand on his back gently as he turned to walk down the street. I noticed a few people headed in our direction and swiftly moved my hand back to my side.

"I thought we might go for a walk," he said, "I hope that's alright."

"It's perfect," I stuttered, "Where to?"

"Oh, I don't know, maybe the park? Green Park, maybe? Or St. James's?"

"Fine. Fine," I said.

We walked back down the street, passing the Gargoyle Club.

"Ever been in there?" I asked him.

"No, it's very exclusive, apparently. Looks amazing from the street, though. All that red reminds me of The Golden," he said, smiling at me, "...can't be as good, though."

We reached Shaftesbury Avenue and headed towards Piccadilly Circus, then down Piccadilly to the Ritz. The street was bustling with lovely ladies in clean-cut dresses and gentlemen scrubbed up to the nines, searching for their next outfit for dinner or dancing. The sun was setting, and the opposite side of the road was bathed in sunlight.

"I'd hate to be one of those models in the window. I'd be burnt right up," I said.

"Let's go down this way," he said, gently tugging at my fingers. He lead me through the gate into Green Park as the evening enveloped the city. It was the kind of cool summer night I always imagined would accompany long strolls with lovers.

"This is my favourite park, I think," he said, "I love the trees over there," he pointed to a small circle of plane trees at the left of the footpath. I noticed a small girl playing with her mother and father, how the mother and father looked at each other whenever the small toddler would fall down or wave a leaf around in triumph. I wondered if I would ever have children. I wondered if I would ever get married. I wondered if Thomas would be in my life longer than the sum of two days.

Thomas seemed troubled, deep in thought; we had been silent ever since we turned onto Piccadilly. He was wearing the same shoes he had worn the night I saw him at The Golden. I imagined he was paying tribute to our first encounter. He had both of his hands in the pockets of his brown overcoat and was watching his feet fall into place in front of him. I took in the scenery above our heads, thinking about how the overhanging branches looked like the Underground map. We came up to the end of Pall Mall by the Palace and stood by the gates for a long time, looking into the windows. I leaned against one of the large stone supports and gazed down the Mall, squinting to make out the face of Queen Victoria.

"Vicky's looking stoic, isn't she?" I said, nudging Thomas with my elbow.

"She is, yes," he said, pivoting quickly to get a look, then turning back to the Palace.

I kicked a small stone by my foot.

"Thomas," I said, "is there something wrong?"

"No, of course not," he said, looking surprised, "there isn't anything wrong."

"It's just," I started, "you haven't been very talkative. I wondered if something was on your mind."

"Oh, yes," he said, "lots of things are on my mind, but nothing's the matter." He looked down the street.

"Why don't we head this way?"

He was gesturing through his pocket with his hand.

I began to feel a bit sick at my stomach.

We began to walk, but before we reached the gate leading into St. James's, I leant against the black balustrade that ran along the walking path and lit a cigarette.

"Want one?" I said.

"Yes," he said, "I'll have one, if that's okay."

"Of course it's okay," I said, "I only share with people I like."

He smiled, avoiding my gaze, and scratched his head. We smoked in silence for several minutes. I finished mine rather quickly, stamping on the butt with my heel. I folded my arms and watched the traffic approach from Trafalgar Square. The

Mall was much quieter than usual. Thomas was watching a duck wobble around a bench and devour a small sandwich that had been left behind. He stood up from the balustrade and was now facing me, looking over my shoulder, toward St. James's park behind me.

After several moments, I said, "Thomas."

"Yes, Henry?" he said, which sounded formal to me.

It was over.

"Would you like me to leave?" I asked.

His eyes widened. It was the first time he had properly looked at me since he had found me on Dean Street.

"No," he said, shaking his head, "Please stay."

"Then what's the matter, Thomas? You haven't said a word for ages."

Thomas was rubbing his forehead with his thumb and his cigarette had gone out. He tried to puff on it unsuccessfully and seemed to despair in something – like he had no other options, no other escape route. He seemed shaken.

"I'm a bit frightened, I suppose," he said, quietly dropping the cigarette.

"Frightened?" I asked, "Why on earth would you be frightened?"

He checked the road for passers-by and took a step toward me. He kissed me on the mouth.

The duck made some sort of noise and I jumped, startled and suddenly brought back to reality. I withdrew from his arms and braced myself against the balustrade. He turned away from me swiftly, covering his face with his hands.

"I'm frightened, Henry," he whimpered, "because I have never in my life encountered someone that makes me feel the way that you do, and I do not know what to do."

A few small tears began to run down his cheek. He covered his face, laughing.

"And the strange thing is," he gasped, "I've only just met you." He turned to look me in the eye and I began to cry as well.

"When we were dancing," he said, wiping his face, "I felt like I was flying. I wished we could have stayed under that table at The Golden for hours."

He lost track of his words and just stood there, looking at me; I felt like I could burst. I let my head drop a little, catching sight, once again, of those same old shoes. He shuffled about a bit, before speaking again.

"Henry?" he asked – I looked up at him — "Please say something."

"I don't know what to say," I said, shrugging helplessly. He frowned and began to furrow his brow before I said, "Other than the fact that I have not stopped saying your name to myself since I left your flat."

I took a breath and exhaled, "And I am frightened, too. I'm terrified."

He straightened up, and sighed, putting both hands over his heart as if to quiet its beating.

"Because," I continued, "you're the most incredible thing that has ever happened to me."

He covered his face and nearly doubled over. He was even more beautiful when he wept.

"When I couldn't remember where your flat was, I thought I had lost you forever," I laughed, "You should have seen me, making wishes on this stupid little conker in hopes that you would find me somehow."

He looked at me, wiping his face. He looked like a child.

"I was so scared you were going to forget about me," he sighed, "I was so scared you were going to forget."

I took his face in my hands and kissed him; tasting his salty tears on his cheek.

"Forget you?" I said, "How could I ever forget you?"

We embraced, both crying and laughing and holding each other tightly before finally coming apart, exhausted. He took my hand and I put my head on his shoulder as we began to walk, keeping vigilant for other civilians in our midst. The small duck had finished his sandwich and was now waddling just behind us. I thought of the mother and father I had seen earlier.

We must have looked like some deranged royal procession: two grown men crying and smiling and wiping their eyes and holding hands with a small duck en train. When we had made our way through the archway at the end of the Mall, I dropped his hand and stopped walking.

"What's the matter?" Thomas asked.

"Nothing. Just being careful."

We both took a small breath before he nodded.

"I so wish I were brave enough to walk down the street holding your hand all the time," I said, "but I get scared."

"Whenever you are frightened," he said, "just hold on tighter."

He took my hand and looked me in the eye.

"Come on," he said, "I know a place."

We walked until the sun was down and made our way to the Strand. Passing the Savoy, I fantasised about a honeymoon in their largest suite, with champagne and hot showers and Thomas, Thomas, Thomas. We held hands the whole evening – he asked me what I was smiling about as we turned down the small corridor which lead to the entrance of The Golden Ballroom. I squeezed his hand.

"Oh, nothing. Just thinking about your *cello lessons*," I said, saluting the doorman. Lindsay was at his normal post, heavily blowing his nose.

"Evening, gents. Just the two?"

"Just the two," said Thomas, smiling at me.

Lindsay raised an eyebrow at me.

"Together or separate?"

Thomas and I exchanged glances.

"Together, please," I blushed.

"Mazel tov," said Lindsay, clicking our token on the desk. We held hands as we passed through the drapes and the corridor; as we approached the second set of drapes, we could hear the band begin to play.

"After you," I said, holding the curtain open.

"Why, thank you," said Thomas, who stole a quick kiss as he went ahead of me.

I smiled at Virginia on the wall.

"I think I love him," I whispered.

The portrait said nothing, but I sometimes recall that she was indeed smiling back at me.

Thomas was on the other side of the curtains, watching the band. I came up behind him and took his hand.

"Beautiful, isn't it?" I said.

He smiled at me, "Yes," he said, taking in the ballroom, "It is a beautiful place, isn't it?"

We watched the couples swirl about the room under the warm light of the chandelier as the smoke billowed and the glass clinked and the music played. I squeezed his hand and he put his head on my shoulder. We were making love right there and then, and we hardly had to touch each other. It was his hair against my face, my fingers locked between his, that sent our souls into the heavens together. We were two shooting stars, forever bonded by the undeniable pull of the planets. I closed my eyes and drew a long sigh as I watched the room waltz around me. We danced for a while before retiring to the same red booth we had discovered on our last visit. With an hour left until closing time, I reminded Thomas of our unopened champagne bottles, and we decided to head back to his flat in Soho, passing through Covent Garden once more, crunching leftover roses under our shoes, to toast London and us and telephone calls and mothers and ballrooms and men and rain and walks in the park. When we reached his front door on Dean Street, he turned to me as he pulled out his keys.

"Remember, now," he said, tapping the front door, "I'm number seventy-seven."

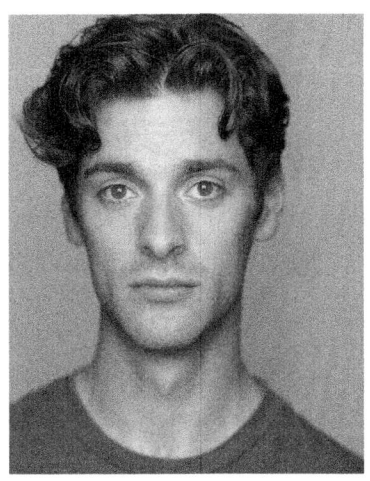

ABOUT THE AUTHOR

Jess Darnell is an actor & poet & artist.

Originally from Nashville, Tennessee, he moved from
sweet tea to high tea to study in London at
The Royal Central School of Speech and Drama.
He is the author of *Only Jewels* and *The Golden Ballroom*,
as well as the creator and host of *Happy Queer Mind*,
an LGBTQ+ self-help podcast.

www.juicethepoet.com
Instagram: @juice.the.poet
Twitter: @juicethepoet

Photo by Wolf Marloh.

Printed in Great Britain
by Amazon

40035202R00047